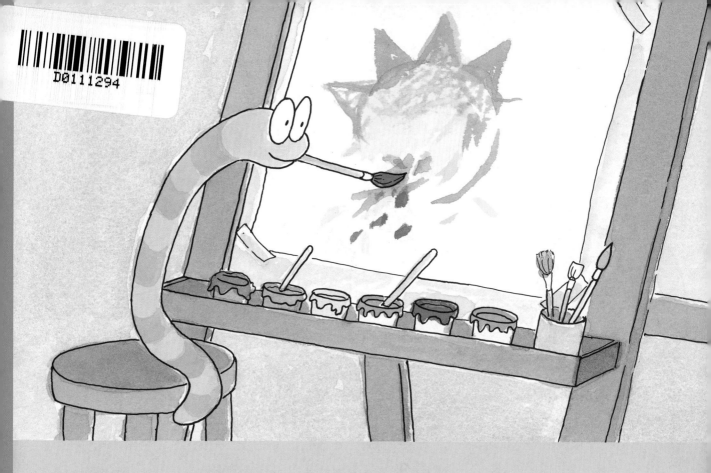

Worm paints a picture.

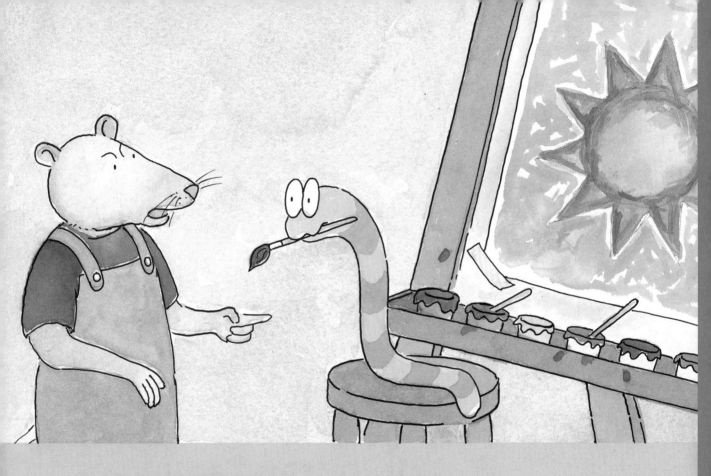

"I don't like it," says Rat.

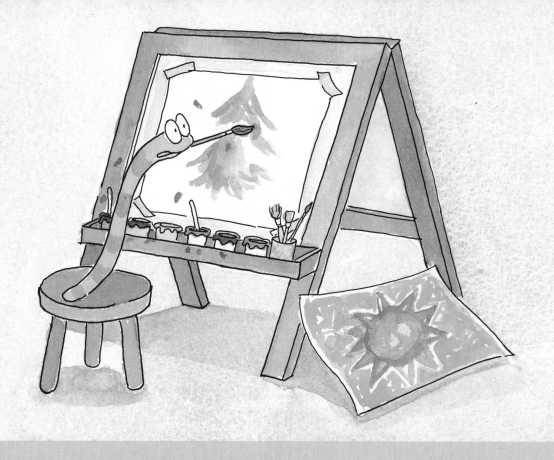

Worm paints a picture.

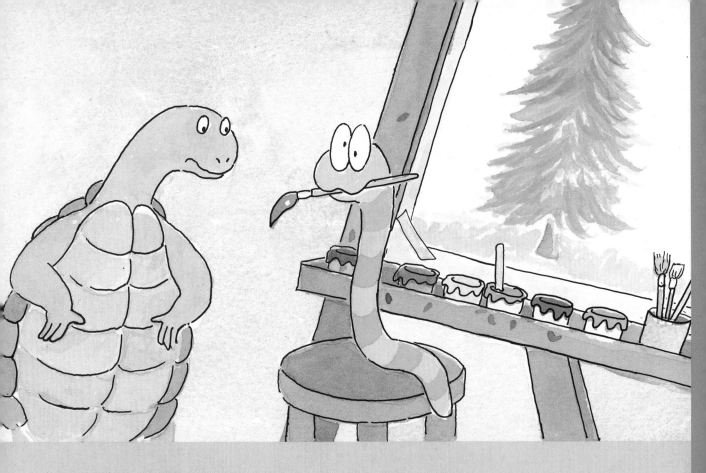

"I don't like it," says Turtle.

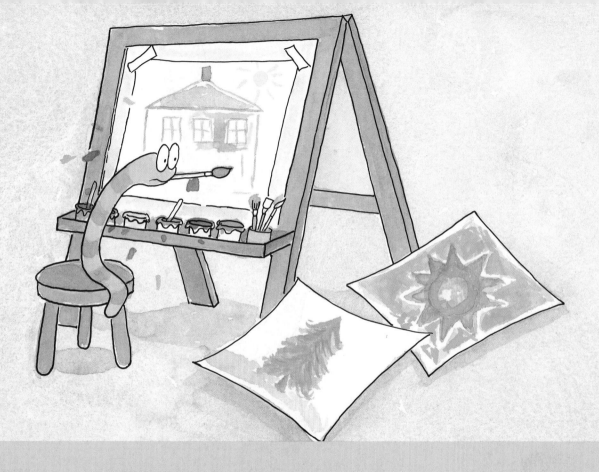

Worm paints a picture.

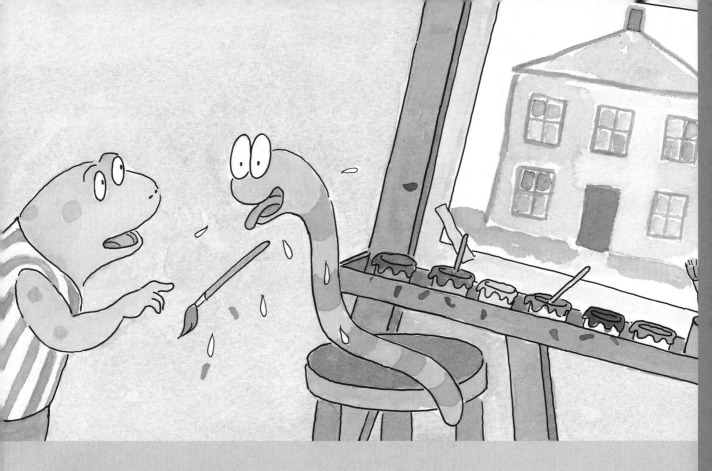

"I don't like it," says Frog.

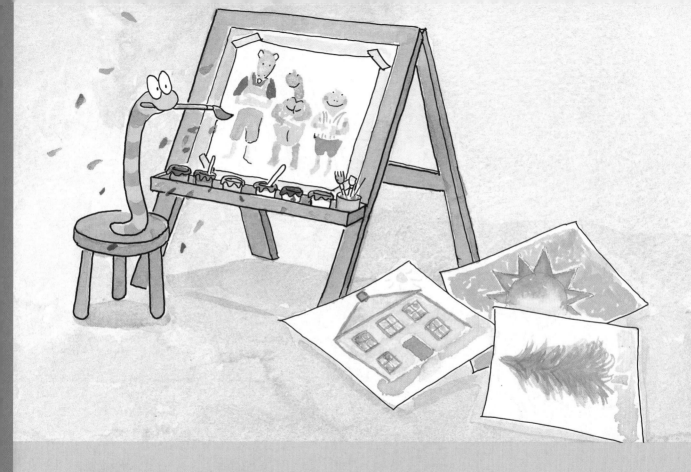

Worm paints a picture.

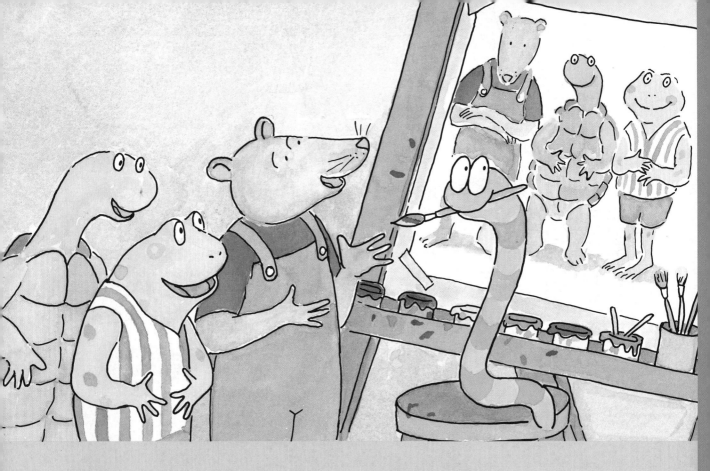

"We love it!" they all say.